7-07

My Father's House

by
Kathi Appelt

illustrated by
Raúl Colón

VIKING

"In my Father's house are many mansions."

John 14:2

For Al Gore, in gratitude for his service and commitment
on behalf of our beautiful blue planet.   —K.A.

For Uncle Frank, for all his words of encouragement.   —R.C.

VIKING
Published by Penguin Group
Penguin Young Readers Group, 345 Hudson Street, New York, New York 10014, U.S.A.
Penguin Group (Canada), 90 Eglinton Avenue East, Suite 700, Toronto, Ontario, Canada M4P 2Y3
(a division of Pearson Penguin Canada Inc.)
Penguin Books Ltd, 80 Strand, London WC2R 0RL, England
Penguin Ireland, 25 St Stephen's Green, Dublin 2, Ireland (a division of Penguin Books Ltd)
Penguin Group (Australia), 250 Camberwell Road, Camberwell, Victoria 3124, Australia (a division of Pearson Australia Group Pty Ltd)
Penguin Books India Pvt Ltd, 11 Community Centre, Panchsheel Park, New Delhi – 110 017, India
Penguin Group (NZ), 67 Apollo Drive, Mairangi Bay, Auckland 1311, New Zealand (a division of Pearson New Zealand Ltd)
Penguin Books (South Africa) (Pty) Ltd, 24 Sturdee Avenue, Rosebank, Johannesburg 2196, South Africa

Penguin Books Ltd, Registered Offices: 80 Strand, London WC2R 0RL, England

First published in 2007 by Viking, a division of Penguin Young Readers Group

1 3 5 7 9 10 8 6 4 2

Text copyright © Kathi Appelt, 2007
Illustrations copyright © Raúl Colón, 2007

LIBRARY OF CONGRESS CATALOGING-IN-PUBLICATION DATA
Appelt, Kathi, date.
My father's house / by Kathi Appelt ; illustrated by Raúl Colón.
p. cm.
ISBN-13: 978-0-670-03669-1 (hardcover)
1. Children's poetry, American. 2. Fathers—Poetry. I. Colón, Raúl, ill. II. Title.
PS3551.P5578M94 2007   811'.54—dc22   2006027630

Manufactured in China • Set in Magna Carta

Oh my Father, thank you,
For all your many mansions . . .

For the one you call the Ocean

With its salted silver spray

Where blue whales snooze in water beds

And flying fishes play.

For the Tundra with its ballroom

Filled with dancing northern lights.

I'll watch the arctic foxes

In their finest coats of white.

And where the trees stand oh so close,
Where deer and rabbits rest,

I'll wander through these Woodland halls
Where songbirds build their nests.

I'll kneel down on your Prairie

Where whippoorwills reside

And feel the wind blow through the grass

And gaze up at the sky.

Oh my Father, thank you . . .

For the Rain Forest with its attic
Where treetops catch the clouds
And spiders catch the raindrops
As they tumble to the ground.

Thank you for the misty Marsh
Where bullfrogs dream all day—
This green and growing nursery
Where baby muskrats play.

I won't forget the Desert
With its painted kitchen walls.

Atop the windblown mesas

Your shy coyote calls.

And Mountains! Oh those mountains!

Their porches wrapped in snow

Where black bears dine on cherries

And watch their bear cubs grow.

For where the river meets the sea,

For pools where starfish hide,

For tides that wash the beaches clean

I'll hold my arms out wide!

I turn my face up toward the sky—
It's the Heavens that I see.
The stars, the moon, the planets,
They're shining down on me.

Oh my Father, thank you
For all your many mansions . . .

I'll keep them fast inside my heart,

For this is what I know . . .

That each and every mansion
Makes this planet we call Home.